Weekly Reader Children's Book Club presents

HILARY KNIGHT'S
The Twelve Days of Christmas

Macmillan Publishing Co., Inc.
New York

This book is a presentation of
Weekly Reader Children's Book Club.

Weekly Reader Children's Book Club
offers book clubs for children from
preschool through junior high school.
For further information write to:
Weekly Reader Children's Book Club
1250 Fairwood Ave.
Columbus, Ohio 43216

for

Katharine
and
Clayton

Joey
&
Betsey

Benjamin
&
Redelia

On the 1st day of Christmas
my true love gave to me:
A partridge in a pear tree.

On the 2nd day of Christmas
my true love gave to me:
Two turtle doves,
And a partridge in a pear tree.

On the 3rd day of Christmas
my true love gave to me:
Three French hens,
Two turtle doves,
And a partridge in a pear tree.

On the 4th day of Christmas
my true love gave to me:
Four calling birds,
Three French hens,
Two turtle doves,
And a partridge in a pear tree.

On the 5th day of Christmas
my true love gave to me:
Five gold rings,
Four calling birds,
Three french hens,
Two turtle doves,
And a partridge in a pear tree.

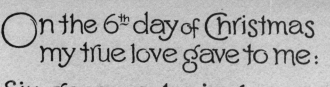

On the 6th day of Christmas
my true love gave to me:

Six geese a-laying,
Five gold rings,
Four calling birds,
Three French hens,
Two turtle doves,
And a partridge in a pear tree.

On the 7th day of Christmas
my true love gave to me:
Seven swans a-swimming,
Six geese a-laying,
Five gold rings,
Four calling birds,
Three French hens,
Two turtle doves,
And a partridge in a pear tree.

On the 8th day of Christmas
my true love gave to me:
Eight maids a-milking,
Seven swans a-swimming,
Six geese a-laying,
Five gold rings,
Four calling birds,
Three French hens,
Two turtle doves,
And a partridge in a pear tree.

On the 9th day of Christmas
   my true love gave to me:
Nine drummers drumming,
Eight maids a-milking,
Seven swans a-swimming,
Six geese a-laying,
Five gold rings,
Four calling birds,
Three French hens,
Two turtle doves,
And a partridge in a pear tree.

On the 10th day of Christmas
my true love gave to me:
Ten fiddlers fiddling,
Nine drummers drumming,
Eight maids a-milking,
Seven swans a-swimming,
Six geese a-laying,
Five gold rings,
Four calling birds,
Three French hens,
Two turtle doves,
And a partridge in a pear tree.

On the 11th day of Christmas
my true love gave to me:
Eleven ladies dancing,
Ten fiddlers fiddling,
Nine drummers drumming,
Eight maids a-milking,
Seven swans a-swimming,
Six geese a-laying,
Five gold rings,
Four calling birds,
Three French hens,
Two turtle doves,
And a partridge in a pear tree.

On the 12th day of Christmas
my true love gave to me:
Twelve lords a-leaping,
Eleven ladies dancing,
Ten fiddlers fiddling,
Nine drummers drumming,
Eight maids a-milking,
Seven swans a-swimming,
Six geese a-laying,
Five gold rings,
Four calling birds,
Three French hens,
Two turtle doves,
And a partridge in a pear tree.